NARRATING IN MY BIRTHDAY SUIT

MAKES "CENTS" TO ME

RACHEL EDWARDS

IREADWARDS PRODUCTIONS LLC

For those wishing to audibly read, tell, and express their own stories. Consider this your invitation to my literal "show and tell." Dress only to impress yourself...gifts need not be wrapped.

MATERNAL NARRATIONS

Tell me a story out of your mouth
So I can fall asleep
With words performed on closed-eyed sets
My cast and future told for me to keep.

— RACHEL EDWARDS

CONTENTS

INTRODUCTION

I'LL WEAR WHAT SHE'S WEARING

Live from *The Scout Awards...Audible's* annual honors for audiobooks, podcasts, and streaming radio...inspired by Harper Lee's legendary narrator Scout Finch in *To Kill a Mockingbird...*

I'm Jana Bakersmith.

For tonight's red carpet, all-star-sounding event coverage, my co-host, Skip Words, joins us from the studio.

Divorce Games Network is thrilled to broadcast this year's gala- where audiences and contenders *literally share* in one another's stories. *The Scout Awards* offer rare opportunities for all of us to match our favorite voices and stories with their entire production casts. The *human beings* behind the microphones...many out of stretchy pants and closet studios for the first time in *months.*

The most talked about story of 2023's *Scout Awards*- isn't even a story...it's the behind-the-sound-production-*process.*

As in how complicated and expensive is the process to make those Audible romance books? What did the narrator have to wear to the studio? Production crew uniforms? Dress codes or freedom-of- fashion expressions?

Let's ask presenter, Rachel Edwards...we hear she narrates a lot of dirty books and tells *all.*

"Great questions, Jana. I'm so far from fancy and more than just a little basic- you *know* know I can't keep secrets. *My voice and eyes tell everything— super "snitchy."* If audiences want the *Down & Dirty* me, I tell them. I'm pretty comfortable in *"my birthday suit"* reading about *"birthday suits, bosoms, and buttocks".* Narrating from a closet at home, it's just like I'm still playing little girl make believe- figuring out how to dress up and act out the parts. *Complete* retail ranger, *shabby-chic-sparkly-farkly...*the thrill of the experience and performance...with a sense of myself. That's just who I am- *inside and out. Narrating in My Birthday Suit is me showing and telling how I played imagination into real life. All my books are written to heard, actually. "*

Well, Skip, I think many of us will want to wear what she's wearing- figuratively or literally, of course. She's wearing her own words and stories.

Our sponsors have asked us to remind audiences *The Scout Awards* does not endorse public nudity, but does support freedom of no pants wearing at home. We encourage contacting licensed trauma therapists and mental health professionals if content presented reveals similar experiences. Explicit language will be used.

— I READ WORDS PRODUCTIONS, 1977-2023

PROLOGUE

MICROPHONE CHECK...TESTING 1,9,8,8

*H*i, hello, how do you do?

I'm here to say a few words to you. My name is Rachel and I'd like to say- I'm running for vice president, today. Responsible. Accurate. Capable-that's me! Honest. Easy-going. And Loyal as can be. So, vote for me when you have the time. 'Cause a check by Rachel's name is the perfect end to my rhyme!

That was 5th grade me...a hot mess of perfectionism, social anxiety, and extreme sensitivity to words- as in the ones people would say when they heard me talk.

And I talked a lot...and read a lot...and wrote a lot- because I had experienced all of those things in the safe embraces of my earliest caregivers- my parents and grandparents.

I was marvelously happy with all the stories in my head.

It just didn't go so well when I tried to get them out of my head...and I spent most of my life-secretly- obsessing over any criticism or negative opinions anyone ever said or wrote to me.

That 5th grade me...she's still here. But this me is now back to that childhood outdoor-porch-stage-planning:

Hi, hello, how do you do?

I'm here to say a few words to you.

My name is Rachel and I'd like to say-

I'm motherfucking awesome- or at least, ok.

Responsible-

Accurate-

Capable- that's me

Honest-

Easy-going-

And Loyal...as can be (obsessively, sarcastically, passively, aggressively, ironically, sexily, nerdily, scandalously, shockingly, morally, and ethically, too).

So, narrate your work when you have the time.

'Cause a lesson learned with Rachel's name,

Is the perfect end to this rhyme.

Allow my prologue to be yours...and please, keep the change.

CHAPTER 1

BEHIND THE SCENES OF AUDIOBOOK CREATION: THE NAKED TRUTH

Birthday Suit Me: Don't say *that* because *they* will judge, take, or reject you. *Restrict* your *words* to avoid trouble, danger, or punishment. So, I learned to make uncomfortable or sensitive topics sound less threatening or offensive. All the time...that's just how I think, write, learn, teach, and live- reflection and projection.

Does this also sound like you? You independently published a romance book. The kind of book that makes you want to read, escape from reality, and hide a provocative cover. A so-called *dirty* book within a exploding self-publishing new frontier?

Social media, fans, and book reviewers tell you about the heat of your work. Your literary and personal voice are described as sexy, authentic, and confident.

Family members, friends, and colleagues are on the fence about your writing- sinful, scandalous, salacious, smut-scribe or sensual, sensational, insightful, intriguing storyteller?

Ludacris, Judy Blume, Jennifer Lopez, Colleen Hoover, Dave Chappelle , Terry McMillan, Shonda Rhimes, Samuel L.

Jackson, Mike Rowe, you say, ready to change the audio narrative.

Are you struggling to reconcile your personal and professional identities? Education and real life? Imposter or influencer?

Are those closest to you waiting to see the sales and lifestyle shifts before making their endorsements known?

You believe in yourself and potential to change the literary landscape.

Except creating the audiobook versions for folks who claim not to read, fans who beg for your voice, not to even mention the stories you are secretly holding, unwritten... how are you supposed to make all *those* happen? Successful authors and scholars should just *know*, right? Storytellers... just *must* be born that way.

Choices, my friends, you have choices. Down & Dirty (basically, Do It Yourself) or a GAT3 in Charlotte, NC (a marvelous professional studio with top of the line recording equipment and sound engineering)...your book, your stories, your voice, your choice.

Would we even be friends? After teaching for 18 years and learning for 46, we learn best from people we generally like or could consider friends- or at least feel connected.

I *am* "Down & Dirty"...and that phrase tends to means stories or experiences I am not sure if I am supposed to talk about or admit experiencing.

There aren't many secrets I care to keep about myself...I *love* money in the bank and getting deals online. There were a lot of words I wasn't *supposed* to say as a "good girl" growing up in Virginia...or a teacher, or a mother...and now, those phrases we said instead actually make me laugh. I had a *"difficult spell"* and *"fucked around and figured out" "airing my dirty laundry" a "dish best served cold"..."some comeuppances".*

Who are we trying to impress?

I'll take real people and stories, any day.

But, that's Birthday Suit Me: Telling Everything About Myself...pretty much vulnerable, and as simple- and comfortable in my skin- as the day I was born...

The hardest step may be knowing where to start. If you want to create an *Audible* for your self-published book, go directly to the acx.com online platform. Select "Authors Who Narrate" and complete your full account profile. All of it. After all, you are living with stories and a voice that wants to be heard.

Birthday Suit Me: I'm just a mom in a closet...reading words off a page...with a dog named Scout. As long as it sounds good and it's what I want, I'll narrate myself...just makes sense after all the years of reading aloud. My closet is nothing compared to reading aloud to middle schoolers and high schoolers ...

CHAPTER 2

HOW TO NARRATE YOUR ROMANCE BOOK
FOR AUDIBLE

*S*ince I *accidentally Audible-ed*, I received some hard lessons when I didn't know all the audio lingo. Not every audiobook is an *Audible*...and not every tissue is a *Kleenex*. Not every audiobook production company does things the same way or uses the same descriptions and prices.

I *learned* the technical parts of *Audible from* the *ACX.com* site and matched feedback from friends and authors. There are some sharp learning curves between "big box" bookstores and the independently published romance fields.

Birthday Suit Me: I felt at home narrating...the dream job I didn't know existed. *Early on, I learned my methods aren't typical and should be reserved for self-narrating authors with similar mindsets and styles to mine.*

Hard lessons are probably the understatement of the century.

Remember the examples I gave you to consider if we would be friends? About narrating your own romance books and getting sideways glances about your work?

I have been "schooled" and "shamed" by more "experts"

than you can imagine... *and I believed them all for at least fifteen minutes each.*

I also have plenty more stories where people seem to like my voice or I enjoyed reading something for others.

So, why should I not narrate my own work and tell other people how? Don't we want authentic voices and books accessible for all? I know I sure do...that's how literacy, literally works.

Just know who you want to be able to hear your books...

Birthday Suit Me: Do You Want To Build An Audible?

Who? An author who has self-published a book.

What? An author who wants to narrate and produce their own audiobook for distribution through *Audible and iTunes.*

When? Their book manuscript is complete and author has rights to publish audiobook version.

Where? *ACX.com* is the development/production website for *Audible.*

Why? You want your book available on *Audible* and narrated by your own voice. Production budget may or may not be a factor in an author's decision. Distribution rights should be carefully read on *ACX's* website.

How? By identifying obstacles holding back your voice, comprehend, and eliminate *Audible*-froster Syndrome.

After setting up a completed account on acx.com, even the most confident authors have a tendency to feel overwhelmed by the production process.

Despite the website having most answers available, the initial barrage of decisions may feel daunting. Use the *ACX* website to reclaim your power- print the requirements for royalties and production of completed audiobook. Whether you are choosing to involve other parties (engineers, studios, narrators) or produce yourself, these resources are significant for a positive experience.

Throughout this short guide, you will experience my stripped down explanations- without entertaining story examples. Basically, the infomercial version. *Overcoming My Audible Frost* should be considered the longer, not-even-anticipated-novella version.

This is the application and practice I use for creating my own audiobooks. This method is designed by someone who feels personal satisfaction accomplishing "do it yourself" projects.

When working with any technology and online platforms, some variations and personal problem-solving should be expected. Every effort has been made to minimize variations between my experiences with the *ACX* platform and audiences intending to create their own audiobooks.

There will always be new technology and platforms in the competitive world of publishing.

Birthday Suit Me: Due to the features and benefits of Audible and its name recognition, I will continue to produce my personal audiobooks through ACX and carefully read all fine print for rights and royalties.

CHAPTER 3

UNLOCKING THE ANATOMY OF AUDIOBOOKS: HOW ANNOTATIONS BRING BOOKS TO LIFE

*N*ot *For The Knowledge:* Aren't you too college-degreed, teaching-certified, or cold, basic white girl to narrate dirty romance books? Or teach others by sharing personal stories? Only if you believe all learning happens in a classroom, with an official textbook, and judged by a test.

In other words, check the 2022 growth statistics for *Audible*...

The fine print decisions of your *ACX* account may require some introspection and forward-thinking. Once you think through who will want to access your audiobook and your overall objective to reach your audience, the fine print should feel livable...at least for now.

Before you start producing your audio files for acx.com (*Audible*), make sure the book manuscript (and copyright) is accessible and able to be added to your account for audiobook development.

The website will offer search options to import from *Kindle* and *Amazon*. Yes, friends, they are all part of the same production "family" and the uploading/publishing experiences will often mirror.

Audiobooks are not intended to include the exact layout as your paperback or ebook. Accomplish this initial content import and preview audiobook expectations/requirements. Save yourself any frustration or surprises during future uploads of audio files. For example, audiobooks on *Audible* currently do not allow sections about the author- an expected standard in paperbacks-and that imported section title will be eliminated and content unnecessary in final upload. So, preserve your time and voice by creating a narration plan correlating requirements for finished audiobook.

AUDIBLE REQUIRES EACH CHAPTER AND SECTION BE RECORDED IN INDIVIDUAL FILES. ONE CHAPTER PER AUDIO FILE.

No matter where you plan to publish your files or record audio for release, check the fine print for expectations, requirements, and distribution copyrights/royalty.

After completing this step, I print a physical copy of my book manuscript. Any portions of printed manuscript not meeting required audiobook outline should be eliminated. Next, I separate each chapter into plastic sleeves and add to a three-ring binder. My annotation process is ridiculously tedious and requires four or five readings per chapter- armed with my favorite highlighters, pens, and pencils.

Naturally, authors already know how they expect a chapter to sound; however, literal readings and voice projections, may only allow a few chapter recordings a day. As an Author Who Narrates, give yourself some grace to learn obstacles that may hinder your project timelines- most of them will depend on your personal schedule, recording environment, and vocal preferences.

If I plan to narrate my own "dirty" book for *Audible*, the

printed, silent, and spoken words will closely align and have similar sounds when read.

There may be some variations with punctuation or text features- because those features exist to communicate an author's intention and meaning to an audience. So, the practices may merge when the author is also the reader and know what they *meant* to write. Remember, when you first started writing and were told to put aside a rough draft to reread with fresh eyes later? Or to then read your writing aloud to catch mistakes? Generally, it is the same concept. But, I digress...

Believe it or not, simply pressing record may cause some nerves and awareness of vocal intonations and word pronunciations not anticipated.

Microphones may pick up sounds you didn't even know your mouth produces with spoken words. No matter how many times you have read your book aloud in book stores, audio equipment and listening to playbacks, may cause some stress.

Our reading experiences and annotation objectives are far more personal than one may expect. Since you do not want to spend hours analyzing every literal breath taken while recording, or editing out pauses that only distract you, find a meaningful method for marking reading notes for narration.

I print each chapter, make narration notes, preview reading lengths, rehearse, and post within recording area for literal reading. That familiarity and repetition also encourages one-take audio-capture and reduces editing needs.

The repeated reading will also allow needed emotions to assist storytelling- or detach, and let the author voice and narrator voice play different roles.

As an author and narrator, choose practices that bring you the most positive experiences.

Birthday Suit Me- I currently choose *Audible* for my audio-book productions, *Spotify* for podcasts, and *Voice Pro 7* for recording audio files. Rachel Edwards, *OCHS '95, EHC '99, UMW '09*, Clayton Tower's mom, and proud furrent to Scout, Katniss, and Bob.

CHAPTER 4

TRIGGER WARNINGS AND READING ADULT CONTENT

An Affair To Remember: If the literary entertainment world only presents affairs as exciting and hot for midlife sexual standards, no wonder many of us are facing relationship reboots in our forties. Traditional self-help books and relationship books of 2020-ish-traditionally-published retailers didn't always meet my personal needs.

TikTok gave me *ACX, BookTok,* and the realization social media platforms were providing content addressing relationship problems that I didn't know others were also experiencing.

As I started working with author Lynn Rhys, her books drew me deep into the steamy bedlands of independently published romances.

Ah, reading stories with characters and plots that felt familiar helped me identify trauma, apply healing strategies, and create emotional resilience...

What's a Trigger Warning?

These are currently added to many independently published books to help readers anticipate content that may cause upsetting emotional reactions or feelings.

After narrating a few for Lynn Rhys and feeling a little like a pharmaceutical commercial of possible side-effects, I asked some questions about their purpose. Authors of self-published works were adding them in an effort to protect their readers by forewarning possible reactions and to seek support of a therapist, if needed. Since traditionally published pieces seem not to carry them and use more of an online motion picture rating system for consumers, my public school educator brain perked up. I reviewed some standard Trigger Warnings with trauma therapist, Karmaria Negron, LCSW. She explained, from a therapeutic perspective, audiences may benefit from having plans to address emotions or memories released during reading...mainly, to pause and consider abandoning a book, continue, or seek a professional to process.

If you are consistently reading and writing about situations that may trigger negative memories, be aware of those feelings and add needed support. Otherwise, you may risk re-traumatizing yourself and not experience a healing narrative process.

But, I digress...and confess.

Ahem, you are going to have to read your written words aloud and record them for your audiobook. So, at the risk of stating the obvious, what will feel most comfortable for you? Do you need to practice certain words to make them sound natural? Plan to record when the family is not home or late at night? Drink some wine? Reading these passages aloud may feel more vulnerable than writing them.

For me: I have never been able to read aloud words that I find personally offensive and not in my personal vocabulary. I also believe in authentic voices for dialect and narration. I guide and discuss books, not censor, control for others, or ban.

I can read and write about intimate sexual encounters. I

can read and write curse words. I also happen to like people and see the best in them. I am comfortable with my own religious faith, personal relationships, and integrity. My moral compass is my own and my loved ones know it.

I sometimes have to compartmentalize narrations before going to church, tell family what not to listen to my work, and say certain words for genitalia about twenty times before reading aloud. I may also read/practice some sections until they are practically voice acting.

But, that's what I have concluded for me...you do whatever you feel is best to achieve your goals.

As a person who didn't truly understand how to develop physical and emotional intimacy in romantic relationships until her forties, I want resources available for others. Even though I loved reading romance books and devoured countless romantic comedies, stories didn't allow me to recognize the self-awareness I lacked to articulate my needs. Intimacy, for me, requires a sensory balance of mind, soul, and body. Until I found my own voice, I was merely performing scripts written for other actors.

Birthday Suit Me: I had to surround myself with a team of professionals and firm deadlines to prevent re-tramautization from repeatedly writing and reading my ex-husband's character descriptions of me. My first ex-husband (yeah, those adjectives are really fun) is a man whom I consider a friend and still family- we are "good divorced"- yep, that's really a thing.

CHAPTER 5

THE ART OF NARRATION: MASTERING THE VARIABLES THAT BRING TEXT TO LIFE

Frosted Cookies: Why should anyone pay a fraud like you for *Audibles* or coaching? Critics of my recording process and inability to describe myself told me to quit sharing my narrations/process. I felt like their words must be true and I was cheating. Or, I was undeserving of compensation for many, many hours of work. Hmmmm... did I know secrets about production or was I just massively insecure? It sure seemed like there was a disconnect between authors, narrators, and production companies.

Birthday Suit Me: When I admitted my feelings to personal business coaches, they supported my work and capacity for success. I might be Down & Dirty, but will only financially cheat myself- which I did over and over. Most likely, my inability to express my voracious need to learn and feel validated professionally- and financially- was hard for others to understand and resulted in unintentionally tapping my feelings of inferiority, insecurity and perfectionism.

We all have our own styles and often are our own hardest critics.

Does anyone know if actors still receive printed scripts or are they all digital now?

No matter how many times I proofread, I still rework after multiple print readings. When I narrate my own pieces, emotions prompt some altered expressions and require freedom for authenticity- if I am anxious about saying single words verbatim, my performance suffers. (When I know I need a professional studio and sound engineer for robust emotional release, I book one. But that's not *Down & Dirty*- just another narration option for authors.)

Most likely, your audience will not be comparing your audiobook and print versions for read aloud; however, sometimes, your spoken word version may feel more authentic.

If aligning words exactly is something you feel passionately about doing, make note that Voice Pro 7 will offer a transcription option- if you want to later update your printed version. Use technology to enhance your voice exposure and objectives, not restrict.

Be aware your audio audience may not have a printed version and traditional skipping ahead or text features may not apply. Vocally, guide your literary audience through your story...

Some stories require a little more to prepare for emotional detachment of narration.

Birthday Suit Me: When producing your own *Audible* for a piece you have self-published, match created audio files with your narration style and *ACX's* requirements.

CHAPTER 6

THE SECRET SAUCES OF AUDIOBOOK NARRATION: REVEALING THE TECHNIQUES

*a*udibles must make and cost a lot of money to produce. *Rachel, you are either living a dream career or are lying to us...something seems off about your stress level.* Everyone had opinions- and eventually, I decided to just share my experiences.

Birthday Suit Me: Early productions and collaborations were all *ACX's* Royalty Shared contracts with authors. I invested in a home printer, *AirPods, WavePad, Voice Pro Full,* and foam pads. I "shopped my apartment" for office supplies, used my *Hewlett-Packard* laptop, and *iPhone.*

Sexy Secret Sauces...aren't. Then again, investing in your vocal vibrations is savoring every drop of your literary essence. Swirl that over your tongue and devour the draughts of word liquors...

Consult *ACX's* audiobook requirements, but this is what currently works for me.

Recording Studio- Determine a comfortable spot to record your chapters or file sections. You must be able to eliminate voice echoes, outside noises, and potential interruptions to your reading. You will also need insulated wall space to post printed chapter pages for narration. I use a corner of an interior bedroom closet and multiple closed doors. The surrounding clothes, blanket wall covering (clothes pins hot-glued, painters' tape connected, printed pages posted per chapter), battery-operated camping lights, and fleece curtain-cloak works well for me. Simply put, find what works to allow best reading experience.

Recording Devices- *Apple iPhone , Apple iPods, Voice Pro 7* (Full version).

Voice Pro 7 Settings- Advanced, MP3, Sample Rate-44,100, Bit Rate-192, Bit Depth-32 , Channel-Mono, Encode Quality-High

Computer- *Hewlett Packard* for *Google Drive, WavePad,* audio files, and *ACX* uploads.

Application- Count quickly to five seconds at beginning and end of each chapter. Read your work the way you want someone to experience it. When you end each chapter, check playback option to make sure audio recorded, change the file title to be recognizable, and upload to *Google Drive.* (Later download to your laptop and edit.)

Google Drive- Download MP3 audio file to laptop.

WavePad- Open desired chapter file downloaded to laptop. (File/Open File)

-Listen to start of the selected raw chapter file. For our purposes, *raw* means unedited and unfinished recording of narrated chapters.

- Adjust/Edit/Effects- Select option to remove background noises. Scan and remove Brief Popping Noises. Next, scan and remove Background Traffic Noises.

-Normalize with- 27.650, -11db, peak loudness rms, preset-simple peak, 3db headroom.

-Save with- Bitrate CBR 192, Mono, High Quality (wait until entire scan is finished to actually save).

Finally, test each completed chapter in ACX's website AudioLab program under Production Resources.

Finished files should be saved until ready for final upload.

Birthday Suit Me: That's definitely *Down & Dirty*...and just what works for me. I do similar things with wardrobe and cosmetic purchases. I find personal satisfaction working at my own pace and exceeding expectations- and competitively saving money doing so.

CHAPTER 7

FROM MANUSCRIPT TO UPLOAD: A COMPREHENSIVE GUIDE TO THE AUDIOBOOK CREATION PROCESS

*M*uch of the self-narration and self-publishing process is- well, independent...and when transitioning from a "by the book" standardized education classroom to the uniquely unstructured *Down & Dirty Me*...I overindulged. As in, I couldn't stop feeling like I had to know *everything* about independent publishing before sharing my experiences.

Figuring out the upload of your completed audio files for *ACX*- clear your morning, friends. No matter how prepared, this step feels like the first bike ride without training wheels. You are *truly* doing this yourself and will overcome all rocks threatening your first production. After a successfully completed audiobook, future rides will feel less daunting and even a little anticlimactic.

From your *ACX* account, select to add your completed audiobook files to produce your *Audible*. Even with your original book's Table of Contents beckoning on the screen, consult the *ACX* requirements. If you upload files that do not meet their requests, your audiobook will be returned for corrections.

Take a deep breath and calmly start transferring your individual audio files. As each file loads, *ACX* programs scan your files for initial compliance. (This is why I use their AudioLab to monitor my own finished files throughout recording journey.)

If any audio files fail during upload process, retrieve the raw audio chapter and complete needed adjustments. I keep all files until finished *Audible* is available on their app (Voice Pro 7,unedited files, and finished files).

Once you have added your finished audio files, clean up Table of Contents- remove category names that will fail approval, create desired chapter titles, and confirm files match each section.

Upload cover art that matches *ACX* requirements.

Finally, submit your completed audiobook for review.

Reward yourself with something...anything...because receiving their congratulatory email and notice quality control reviewers now have your voice within their checking software...may not quite satisfy your sense of accom-plishment.

You now have three to ten business days to wonder about those *Quality Control Gods*.

Birthday Suit Me: Yes, yes I am *Team Fuck Around And Figure It Out. I also hold my breath each time I send any files through AudioLab...so I do it with everything now. Ridiculous, but it sure builds my confidence and self-esteem.*

CHAPTER 8

BREAKING IT DOWN: THE ESSENTIAL GUIDE TO AUDIOBOOK ECONOMICS

*Q*uality *Control Gods* aren't satisfied. *Well, shit.* Something needs to be changed and resubmitted for *ACX* to approve your audiobook for *Audible*. Sometimes, despite best efforts, an email will arrive returning your audiobook for corrections.

Audible Froster!! Imposter Alert...Imposter Alert....nah, that's just what my brain did the first few times.

Even though you may feel frustrated and confused, carefully read the entire email and determine the actionable steps needed for execution. Don't take it as a personal affront to your character or voice.

Quality Control Gods are just using more intense software to match files to standards- with the number of *Audible* books currently on the market, I highly doubt they are "listening" to all our hours of reading. Make the needed adjustments from your *raw* audio files or cover art measurements and resubmit for review. If you attempt to adjust finished audio files, your overall sound will shift- not a great sound, at all.

Technology sometimes just *is awkward.*

Birthday Suit Me: Reframing, personifying, and giving character traits to technology and life just *sounds* more interesting, doesn't it?

Audible Frost ends with a pinging email alert.

Publication and availability of your *ACX* audiobook through *Audible* and iTunes, arrives with a simple email notice. Your hard work will magically be accessible for preview, purchase, download, and distribution.

You will also receive a second email notice announcing access to your free downloads to distribute. Surprise! Typically, in my experience, each title receives about fifty...but, some platform variations may change over time.

Still, I always love this feature. Explore the *ACX* dashboard and your profile to access promo codes, track sales, downloads, and royalty payments. As you copy and paste codes to family and friends, remember to slide the toggle bar to keep track of the shares.

Whether that happens on business day four or ten, the feeling of accomplishment must come from within *you*. Is it a big deal? Absolutely. But, maybe, the world won't immediately recognize how much work you put into receiving that notice of acceptance.

Congratulations! Celebrate.

Just as you did with your first printed or published work, design a plan to share your voice with others. Direct all the traffic you want to your new audiobook- new ways are developing all the time.

Without downloading your book, previews allow your storytelling voice to be heard- that's also why selecting that section was so important for audiobook design. First impressions tend to *sell* a book. Direct sharing from within the *Audible* app to text messages may be an appealing way to encourage those who are technology hesitant.

Who will receive your announcements? Fun instructions for how to listen, learn, and experience your work?

Finding new ways to share your voice and stories are all part of the excitement.

Prices for *Audible* subscriptions, downloads, and royalties will continue to wiggle as the market continues to grow. Frequently check the app itself for new features, hiccups, and marketing ideas. You may also notice some royalty payment differences between platform families (*Kindle Direct Publishing, Amazon, ACX, Kindle, etc.*)

If you are already in the self-publishing worlds, you already realize new digital babies and programs are birthed almost daily.

More than anything else, take some time to celebrate your voice. If everyone knew how to produce their own *Audibles,* I doubt there would be so many big companies charging big money to do it for you.

But what do I know? Just makes sense and "c-e-n-t-s" to try my method before spending money you may never recoup.

Birthday Suit Me- There is really nothing like the first time you hear your own voice on *Audible.* Since the platform is so popular, remember to connect your *Alexa,* share through iPhone, social media, and email.

CHAPTER 9

2023 SCOUT AWARDS BIRTHDAY SUIT COLLABORATIONS

he Scout Awards Show. Audible's annual celebration honoring audiobooks, podcasts, and streaming radio- inspired by Harper Lee's legendary narrator, Scout Finch, in *To Kill A Mockingbird.*

Rachel Edwards's Narration Highlights in Order of Audible Release:

In the categories of Romance and Dark Romance:

Nothing Like Him, Jessica Roe:

"I didn't know if I was imagining it due to the whole almost dying thing, but to me it felt like there was some epic vibage going on between the two of us. It almost seemed...it almost seemed like he was looking at me in the exact same way I was looking at him. Could it be?"

Scars On My Heart, Lynn Rhys-

"Here's the thing. It's not that I refuse to change, it's just that I refuse to change for you. This is me. This is who I am. Instead of focusing on me, telling me how beautiful I would look only if I would make changes, how about you change your shitty attitude? I'm not changing for fucking anybody."

Safe with Me, Lynn Rhys-

"His jaw is strong and square, his cheekbones high. He has tattoos up and down his left arm, and his shirt hugs every muscle on him- and boy, is he ripped. His hair's dark and cut short on the top and shaved on the sides. This man is sex on legs. He's tall, dark, and fucking handsome."

Neighbors, Lynn Rhys-

"Our tongues dance, igniting the fire that has been blazing between us for so long. Right at this very moment, we connect our souls. Our hearts beat rapidly against each other, and our lips convey everything we don't say. This is the beginning of everything. The beginning of us."

Treasure Found, Tim Grossi-

"That trip was headed for Fredericksburg. After unloading and during their overnight stay, Virgil had been regaled with stories of the gold mines in Spotsylvania, Fauquier, and Louisa Counties."

From the Ashes, Lynn Rhys-

"I roll my eyes. 'No, you asshole. Normal high school has normal fucking terrible food. Rubber, bland chicken nuggets and canned fruit. Oh, and square pizza every Friday.' I can't even believe what I'm looking at. My eyes don't know where to look first. 'This is seriously the school dining hall?'

'Yeah, it is. Welcome to Darkwood. Though I'm sure more surprises await,' she says mysteriously.

From the Darkness, Lynn Rhys-

"Is there such a thing as a food and sex coma? If so, I am definitely having one of those right now. Also, I may be burning up, but that is solely because I'm surrounded by my men. My Kings."

Birthday Suit Me: Each title is a winner in its own way for lessons learned narrating. However, *From the Darkness*, produced some particularly cathartic moments. For that reason, expect more recognition for Lynn Rhys and personal analysis by Rachel Edwards in *Overcoming My Audible Frost: The Down & Dirty.*

EPILOGUE

OVERCOMING MY AUDIBLE FROST

elling Stories Out Of My Mouth: You need *how* much money this month? For about a year and a half, I relied on my parents to help establish my life and achieve the "What the Frox?" divorce...and I both appreciated and resented needing those checks. By the final months, I could feel the final *Audible Frost* leave my body *and* trace its roots. As I typed pieces for my own first book drafts, my mind started playing unwritten stories- many of which I had failed to complete over the last 40 years. I always loved my mother's "stories told out of her mouth"... and hadn't realized the need to find my identity as an author.

After the past year and what could be viewed as immeasurable personal and professional growth, what obstacles could prevent publishing and distributing my own stories? The ones about my life and the incredible people whom I have been fortunate to know. Moving through paralyzing manipulation by "froxic relationships" to the *"absolute intimacy"* of narrating my mind?

Only one...and that obstacle was me...I was the one who was "holding out for validation, encouragement, or recognition"...from individuals undeserving of that power over my voice.

But first, I better tell you *The Down & Dirty* parts of what *really* frosted a lot more than *just* cookies or *my* voice.

The voice in my head telling me to shut my mouth and run...

Overcoming My Audible Frost: The Down & Dirty will answer all questions raised within and help give amends. But for now, I will just say...

The End.

www.ingramcontent.com/pod-product-compliance
Lightning Source LLC
Chambersburg PA
CBHW020616130626
46552CB00015B/3100